To:

W0037654

From:

once

a

storm

once

BY JANET TRULL

a

ILLUSTRATIONS BY M. C. JOUDREY

storm

AT BAY
press

WINNIPEG

Once a Storm

Copyright © 2020 Janet Trull

Design by M. C. Joudrey and Matthew Stevens.
Layout by Matthew Stevens and M. C. Joudrey.

Published by At Bay Press May 2020.

Library and Archives Canada cataloguing in publication is available upon request.

ISBN 978-1-988168-29-6

Printed and bound in Canada.

This book is printed on acid free paper that is 100% recycled ancient forest friendly (100% post-consumer recycled).

First Edition

10 9 8 7 6 5 4 3 2 1

atbaypress.com

once a storm

There once was a little girl who perceived her path in life to be difficult.

How could she live up to the world's
high expectations?

She felt heavy and clumsy and
unbeautiful and she thought others judged
her as harshly as she judged her own reflection.

She could not leave her home without tripping
over the underbrush of self-loathing.

Convinced there must be an easier way to travel through life, she set off on her own.

She searched in forests until she was covered in scratches and insect bites.

She walked on damaged roads that left her tender feet cut and bleeding.

Her friends and family called to her from paths that were smoother and brighter, but she mistrusted their motivations and maintained her treacherous journey.

The girl grew up and found other sufferers who had much to teach her about the ways of feeling better.

Relief bubbled up in her heart and the beauty of it flowed through her veins.

Finally, she belonged.

Then out of nowhere, the storm hit.

She stumbled along in the fog and rain from one dim path to the next, following travelers who claimed to know the way.

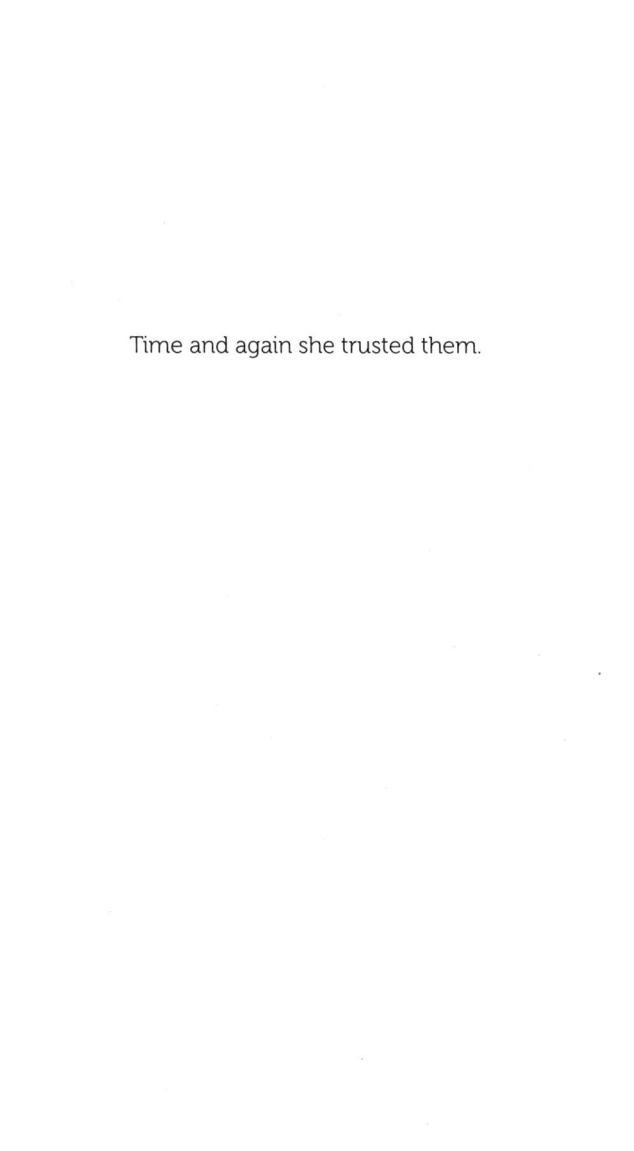

Time and again she trusted them.

Time and again, she was abandoned on slopes so hopelessly slippery that she had no traction at all.

Out of control, she slid for the longest time, grabbing at twigs, clinging to rocks, until she was immersed in rushing water.

The terror was exhilarating.

Just as she expected to be swept away forever,
a reprieve.

Drifting into a quiet bay, she could hear the birds singing, smell the honeysuckle, feel the sand under her feet.

She understood clearly that she was
going to be all right.

Upriver, her family and friends waded in the cold water, waving and welcoming.

They had already risked much to get her back, and they were willing to do more, but she would have to do the hard work of swimming against the current.

She had once been a strong swimmer and her muscles remembered the satisfaction of the front crawl.

Arm over arm.

Head turning to see her progress in relation to the shore.

Oh, but her arms got tired.

You can do it, her father called.

NO, I CANNOT!

You're strong, her mother screamed.

NO I AM NOT!

We love you, her friends yelled.
QUIT SAYING THAT!

What harm if she floated on her back for a while?

The clouds were lovely, wispy and delicate as she relaxed and let the water carry her to the brink of the falls.

The girl reveled in the explosive adrenaline of danger, and gave into the power of it.

Enraptured, she danced.

And then she was gone.

The river flows on, delivering messages of grief.

Of memory. Of hope.

Changing the landscape slowly but forever.

After the drama of the waterfall and the helpless ride through the whirlpool, addicts wash up on the shore like pebbles.

Grab a handful.

They are unique and precious and, too easily, they slip through our fingers.

Dedicated to Katie Danielle Paré
March 2, 1990 ~ March 15, 2014

Once a peaceful, loving child.
Once a teenager suffering from anxiety.
Once a young adult addicted to Oxycontin.
Once a victim of accidental overdose.
Forever a blue-eyed angel.

Janet Trull, freelance writer with a regular column in *The Haliburton County Echo*, one of the last privately owned newspapers in Ontario. Her personal essays, professional writing in the education field, and short stories have appeared in *The Globe and Mail, Canadian Living Magazine, Prairie Fire, The New Quarterly* and *subTerrain Magazine*, among others. She won the CBC Canada Writes Challenge, Close Encounters with Science, in 2013 and was nominated for a Western Magazine Award in the short fiction category in 2014. *Hot Town and Other Stories* her first collection of short stories, was released from At Bay Press in 2016.

M. C. Joudrey, Canadian writer, artist, and designer. His collection of short stories, *Charleswood Road: Stories*, received a Manitoba Book Awards nomination for Most Promising Writer. He has been a member of the selection committee for the CBC Short Fiction Prize and a jury member for the Manitoba Book Awards. He is also a bookbinder with works held in various galleries internationally.

Other books in the "From the Heart" series.

you

LYRICS BY DRIVIN' N CRYIN'

mean

ILLUSTRATIONS BY M. C. JOUDREY

everything